Contents

*Levels**	*Title*	*Composer*	*Page*
S B	**Camel Ride**	Paul Harris	2
S B	**Beach Combing**	Sarah Watts	3
S (B)	**Minuetto** from Divertimento in C, K. 187	attrib. Mozart arr. Paul Harris	4
S S	**Swing low, sweet chariot**	Spiritual arr. Robert Hinchliffe	5
S S	**Two Go Blues**	Alan Haughton	6
S G	**Bun-Fight at the O.K. Corral**	Sally Adams	7
S S B	**The Old Banger**	Paul Harris	8
S S S	**The Mysterious Mr Fox**	Pam Wedgwood	10
S S S	**Matilda's Wedding**	Trad./Wagner arr. Paul Harvey	12
S (S) (S)	**This old man, he played swing!**	Trad. arr. James Rae	14
S S (B) (B)	**Dozing under a Coconut Tree**	Paul Harris	16
S S S S	**Country Gardens**	Trad. English arr. Paul Harvey	18
S S (S) (S)	**Are we there yet?**	Sarah Watts	20
S S G G	**Viva! Viva!**	Brian Chapple	22

*B = bronze; S = silver; G = gold; ( ) = the line must be played but cannot be assessed for a Medal.

Camel Ride

Paul Harris

Beach Combing

Sarah Watts

Minuetto

from Divertimento in C, K.187

attrib. Mozart arr. Paul Harris

Swing low, sweet chariot

Spiritual arr. Robert Hinchliffe

Two Go Blues

Alan Haughton

Moderate swing (♩♩ = ♩ ♪ in triplets) ♩ = *c.*114

Bun-Fight at the O.K. Corral

Sally Adams

The Old Banger

Paul Harris

13
. . . another near miss!
sfz
sfz
sfz
17
mf
mf
mf
21
It backfires
24
. . . and splutters to a stop.

The Mysterious Mr Fox

Pam Wedgwood

12
16
19

Matilda's Wedding

Trad. and Wagner arr. Paul Harvey

13
f
f
mf
mf
17
f
f
20
p
p
p

This old man, he played swing!

Trad. arr. James Rae

Cool swing feel (♫ = ♩♪ triplet) ♩ = *c.* 140

14
f
f
f
18
mf
mf
mf
22
f
f
f

Dozing under a Coconut Tree

Paul Harris

13
18
23

Country Gardens

Trad. English arr. Paul Harvey

13
mf
f
17
f
p
mf
f
21
mf
f

Are we there yet?

Sarah Watts

13
mf
mf
mf
mf

17

to my grandson, John

Viva! Viva!

Brian Chapple

12
mf
mf
mf
mf
16
20
f
mf
mf
f
mf
mf

24
cresc.
cresc.
cresc.
cresc.
28
f
f
f
f
32